Exploring Science

The Exploring Science series is designed to familiarize young students with science topics taught in grades 4–9. The topics in each book are divided into knowledge and understanding sections, followed by exploration by means of simple projects or experiments. The topics are also sequenced from easiest to more complex, and should be worked through until the correct level of attainment for the age and ability of the student is reached. Carefully planned Test Yourself questions at the end of each topic allow the student to gain a sense of achievement on mastering the subject.

EXPLORING
VARIETY OF LIFE

Robert Stephenson
and
Roger Browne

Illustrated by Marilyn Clay

RSVP
RAINTREE
STECK-VAUGHN
PUBLISHERS
The Steck-Vaughn Company
Austin, Texas

Exploring Science

Earth in Space
Electricity
Energy Sources
Forces and Structures
Habitats
The Human Body
Humans and the Environment
Information Technology

Light
Magnets
Plants
Soil and Rocks
Sound
Uses of Energy
Variety of Life
Weather

Library of Congress Cataloging-in-Publication Data

Stephenson, Robert, 1950–
    Exploring variety of life / Robert Stephenson and Roger Browne;
  illustrated by Marilyn Clay.
        p.   cm. — (Exploring science)
      Includes index.
      Summary: Describes life on Earth, from bacteria and algae to
  reptiles, birds, and mammals, and discusses classification,
  evolution, extinction, and genetics.
      ISBN 0–8114–2606–8
      1. Biology—Juvenile literature.   [1. Biology.]   I. Browne,
  Roger, 1946–   . II. Clay, Marilyn, ill.   III. Title,   IV. Series.
  QH309.2.S76   1993   92-34357
  574—dc20   CIP
                                                        AC

Cover illustrations:
Above A group of Burchellis zebras in Africa.
Below right A dark-green fritillary (nymphalid butterfly) takes nectar from a flower.
Below left A diagram to show part of an insect's breathing mechanism.
Frontispiece Puffballs are a type of fungus. As raindrops fall on these ripe puffballs, they shoot out spores from which new puffballs can grow.

Editor: Elizabeth Spiers
Editor, American Edition: Susan Wilson
Designer: Marilyn Clay
Series designer: Ross George

Typeset by Multifacit Graphics, Keyport, NJ
Printed in Italy by G. Canale & C.S.p.A., Turin
Bound in the United States by Lake Book, Melrose Park, IL

1 2 3 4 5 6 7 8 9 0 Ca 97 96 95 94 93 92

Contents

What Is a Living Thing?   6
Simple Life   10
Classification   12
Plants   16
Decomposers   18
Simple Animals   20
Mollusks   22
Arthropods   24
Fish   28
Amphibians and Reptiles   30
Birds   32
Mammals   34
Evolution and Extinction   38
Genetics   42

Glossary   46
Books to Read   47
Index   48

WHAT IS A LIVING THING?

There is an enormous variety of living things on Earth. Living things are found almost everywhere—in the hottest desert, the deepest ocean, and the snows of the polar ice caps. And there is an astonishing variety of shapes, colors, and sizes. The smallest living things, such as bacteria, are visible only under a microscope. The largest include the elephant, which is a massive 6 tons, and the giant sequoia tree, one of the largest living things.

What is a living thing? Most things are obviously alive or not alive—a person is a living thing and a rock is not. But sometimes the answer is more complicated. For example, a virus, has some traits of living things but not others. To tell living things from nonliving, scientists have identified seven functions of all living things. The seven functions are described below. For something to be identified as a living thing, it must have all these functions.

Living things need food for growth, repair, and energy.

FOOD-GETTING

Like people all other living things need food. Food provides the raw materials needed for growth, energy, and good health. Living things get their food in a great number of different ways. For example, plants use sunlight to make their own food, while animals must take in food by eating plants or other animals.

RESPIRATION

Food contains energy. But before this energy can be used, it must be released. The process of releasing energy from food is called respiration. You may have heard this term before—breathing is another type of respiration. Both types take in oxygen, a gas found in air. For energy to be released, simple foods, called sugars, combine with oxygen. Sugar is broken down to form carbon dioxide gas and water. As a result of this breakdown of sugar, energy is released for use in life processes.

WASTE REMOVAL

Life processes often produce wastes. For example, when an animal eats, not all parts of its food can be broken down and used. The process of respiration also produces wastes. If these wastes were not removed, they would poison and eventually kill the living thing.

Above *Tulips have an underground bulb of closely packed leaves full of stored food. Above ground the flowers and leaves will die off, but a new plant will grow from the bulb, when conditions are right.*

GROWTH AND REPAIR

All living things grow. To grow, they use building materials found in their food. Animals tend to grow to a particular size, while others, such as plants, may continue growing throughout their lives. But at all stages of life, living things use these same building materials to repair parts that are damaged or worn out. Growth and repair are both ongoing processes.

MOVEMENT

All living things move. For example, plants move as they grow towards a light source, such as the sun. Animals move to catch food or to escape from danger. Living things get their energy for movement from their food.

SENSITIVITY

All living things are sensitive to changes around and within them. For example, there may be changes in temperature, light, or the need for food. Living things react in some way to these changes, such as by quickly moving away from a hot object.

This venus flytrap has special cells that are sensitive to touch. When the fly walks across the cells, the leaves will snap shut.

REPRODUCTION

Because they do not live forever, all living things make new "copies" of themselves. This is called reproduction. Some organisms make exact copies of themselves by asexual reproduction. Others carry out sexual reproduction in which a sperm, or male sex cell, and an egg, or female sex cell, join together. The young that is pro-

__Above__ Every living thing must produce offspring so that its species can survive. These baby elephants were produced by sexual reproduction.

duced from this union of egg and sperm will be similar to, but not exactly like its parents. Only living things of the same species are able to mate, or reproduce, by sexual reproduction.

Right *Fungi like these reproduce by asexual reproduction.*

Living things share the world with things that are not living. Nonliving things include things that were once living, such as the vegetables we eat, as well as things that have never lived such as rocks and metal. For an object to be alive, it must have all seven functions of living things. (These functions are described on pages 6, 7, and 8.) For example, a car takes in energy in the form of gasoline and burns it in a process similar to respiration. It gets rid of waste in its exhaust gases. It moves, but it cannot reproduce or grow, and it only responds to change if its driver does.

ACTIVITY

YOU NEED

a large range of objects—try to include:
- **a plant bulb**
- **a rock**
- **dried peas**
- **a plastic spoon**

1 Work with a friend.
2 Make a chart with 3 columns.

never alive	dead	living

3 Look at each object. Try to decide whether it is living, dead, or has never been alive. Write down or draw the object in the correct column.
4 To which columns do you think the following belong?
- a flame
- water
- a piece of leather
5 Think of some more living, dead, or never-alive things and add them to your lists.
6 If there are any objects that you are not sure about, write down why. Ask people in other groups what they think.

TEST YOURSELF

1. How many different tasks must every living thing carry out?
2. Which of the following are living, non-living, or have never lived?
   - a wooden chair   • a coin   • starfish   •raisins

SIMPLE LIFE

All living things are made up of tiny building blocks called cells. The more complicated the living thing is, the more cells of different types it has in its body.

Scientists have found evidence that life began on Earth about 3.5 billion years ago. The earliest living things were made up of only one cell. There are still many single-celled forms of life living very successfully on Earth today. What follows is a description of these simple forms of life.

BACTERIA

Bacteria can be found almost anywhere on Earth—in very hot and very cold places, at the bottom of the deepest ocean, even on and inside other living things. They can feed on an enormous number of different things. A bacterium is made up of a single, very simple cell surrounded by a rigid wall. Food and gases such as oxygen pass into its body through the cell wall, and waste passes out in the same way.

Bacteria affect the lives of other living things in ways both helpful and harmful. For example, you have millions of bacteria in your intestines that help to break down fruits and vegetables that you eat. But certain bacteria can cause diseases such as whooping cough, tuberculosis, cholera, or other contagious diseases.

ALGAE

This is the simplest group of plant-like living things and it has many members that are one-celled. They all live in water and are rather like bacteria, having very simple, rigid-walled cells. Algae were among the first living things to appear on the planet Earth.

PROTISTS

Although protists are one-celled living things, their cells are more complicated than those of bacteria or some algae. Protists may have the traits of plants or animals or both. Some protists live in water, others live in the soil, while many live inside the bodies of other animals. Protists are usually parasites and can cause disease and sometimes death. Diseases they cause include malaria, dysentery, and sleeping sickness.

These protists are single-celled life-forms.

ACTIVITY

INVESTIGATING ALGAE

YOU NEED

- **a jam jar**
- **string**
- **a pond**
- **black paper, large enough to cover the jar**
- **cellophane tape**

WARNING: Never go to a pond alone. Always tell an adult where you are going.

- **a cotton swab**
- **a microscope slide with cover slip**
- **a strong hand lens or microscope**

1 Tie a piece of string around the neck of the jam jar. Lower it into the pond to collect a sample of water.

2 Using the black paper and the tape, make a tube to fit around the jar. Make a small hole in the side of the black paper tube.

3 Leave the jar with its tube in a bright place for 2 to 3 hours.

4 Remove the tube. You should see some green scum on the jar where the hole in the tube was. Carefully pour the water back into the pond.

5 Remove the green scum from the jar using a cotton swab. Wipe the swab on the microscope slide. Add a drop of water to the green scum, using the cotton swab again. Put the cover slip over the water and the green scum.

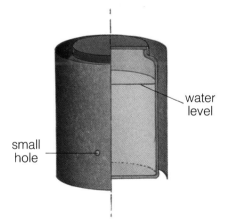

water level

small hole

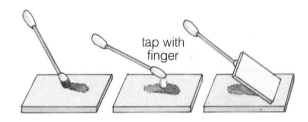

tap with finger

6 Look at the green scum through the hand lens. Can you see the cells? Draw what you can see. The green scum that you see here is algae.

TEST YOURSELF

1. What is the name of the tiny building blocks that make up a living thing's body?

2. How do bacteria get food and gases such as oxygen?

3. What are protists?

CLASSIFICATION

You have already found out about some groups of living things. Before you look at some more, it is important to know how to find out what a particular living thing is. Biologists, the scientists who study living things, have sorted them into different groups to make them easier to identify and study. This sorting process is known as classification.

The first step in classifying a living thing is to carefully observe it. A scientist would identify traits such as the color, size, and shape, as well as the actions of a living thing. Using these traits, biologists classify, or group, similar things together.

Biologists start by dividing living things into kingdoms. You may have heard of two of them—the plant kingdom and the animal kingdom. The other kingdoms are the bacteria, protists, and fungi. Protists include one-celled living things such as the amoeba. Fungi include toadstools, mushrooms, and molds.

A kingdom is then divided up into large groups called phyla. The living things in a phylum have the same basic body plan. A phylum is further divided up into classes. Living things in the same class are much more alike than those in the same phylum. Classes are then divided up into orders. The charts on the next two pages show how the animal kingdom is classified.

Here are two simple examples to show you how to use the classification keys: a dog and a spider. A dog has a backbone, so it is a VERTEBRATE. It is warm-blooded, breathes air using lungs, has body hair, and feeds its young with milk produced from the mother's body. This means it is a MAMMAL. It is a CARNIVORE (meat-eater).

A spider is an animal without a backbone—an INVERTEBRATE. It has a hard outer skin, a segmented body, and jointed legs, so it is an ARTHROPOD. It has four pairs of legs, so it is an ARACHNID.

Millipedes are invertebrates. They have jointed legs, a segmented body, and a hard skin—this means they are arthropods. This millipede lives on the forest floor in Venezuela and is active mostly at night.

Invertebrates - animals without backbones

starfish

jellyfish

sea mat

Echinodermata
- animals with tough spiny skins
- their bodies have parts arranged in five or in multiples of five

Coelenterata
- soft, jelly-like animals with hollow bodies
- they catch prey on stinging tentacles

Bryzoa
- tiny animals that live in colonies enclosed in stony tubes or sheets
- moss animals cannot move, but they filter-feed using a circle of tentacles

Porifera
- animals with stiff bodies
- sponges filter-feed through their bodies
- water enters and leaves through a series of holes called pores

sponges

Nematoda
- simple animals with tube-shaped bodies
- commonly called roundworms
- covered by a thick cuticle that molts as the animal grows
- include free-living and parasitic worms

hookworm

INVERTEBRATES

Platyhelminthes
- simple animals whose gut has only one opening—the mouth
- flatworms have no blood circulation

flatworms

Annelida
- have a mouth and an anus
- they have a well developed blood circulation

earthworms

Mollusca
- soft-bodied animals often surrounded by a hard shell or shells
- squids and octopuses may have the shell inside the body
- internal organs are usually covered with a mantle—a folded sheet of tissue

Arthropoda
- animals with jointed legs
- have a hard skin or shell called the cuticle
- the body is divided into segments

Brachiopoda
- lamp shells have a pair of shells joined by a hinge
- they filter-feed using a ring of tentacles in between the two shells

ant

spider

lamp shell

landsnail

octopus

Vertebrates - animals with backbones

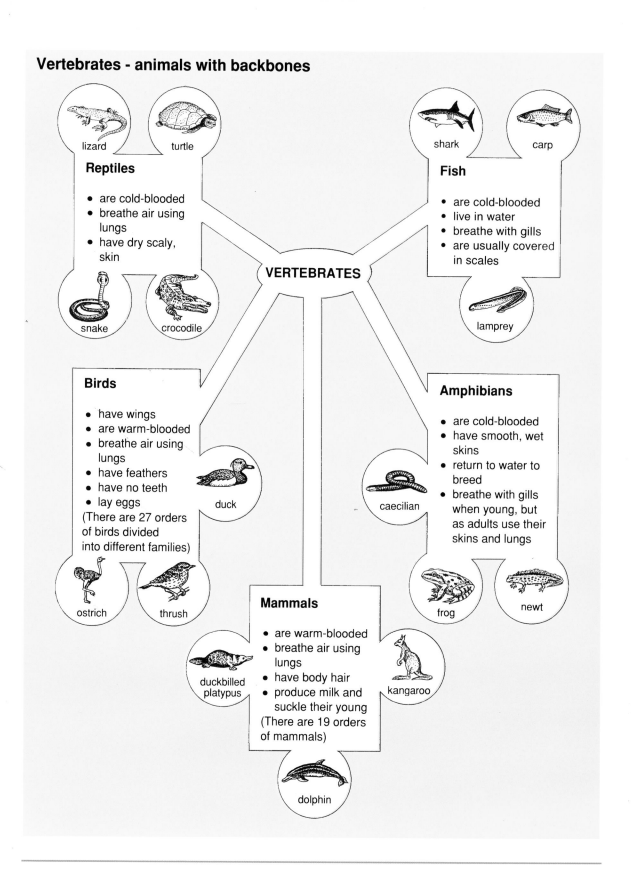

Reptiles

- are cold-blooded
- breathe air using lungs
- have dry scaly, skin

lizard

turtle

snake

crocodile

Fish

- are cold-blooded
- live in water
- breathe with gills
- are usually covered in scales

shark

carp

lamprey

VERTEBRATES

Birds

- have wings
- are warm-blooded
- breathe air using lungs
- have feathers
- have no teeth
- lay eggs

(There are 27 orders of birds divided into different families)

duck

ostrich

thrush

Amphibians

- are cold-blooded
- have smooth, wet skins
- return to water to breed
- breathe with gills when young, but as adults use their skins and lungs

caecilian

frog

newt

Mammals

- are warm-blooded
- breathe air using lungs
- have body hair
- produce milk and suckle their young

(There are 19 orders of mammals)

duckbilled platypus

kangaroo

dolphin

An owl has a backbone so it is a vertebrate. It is warm-blooded, has wings, feathers, and lays eggs, which means it is a bird. It is also a carnivore or meat-eater.

ACTIVITY

1 Try to fit the animals in the list below into the classification keys shown on pages 13 and 14:
  • a tapeworm
  • an elephant
  • a ladybug
  • a goldfish

2 Use the classification key to show you what you need to know about each animal. Look for clues about these animals in the natural history section or encyclopedias in the library.

3 Ask a friend to think of a few more animals to try.

4 Display your classification keys for each animal as shown in the example.

Example: lion and garden spider

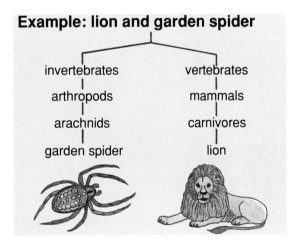

invertebrates	vertebrates
arthropods	mammals
arachnids	carnivores
garden spider	lion

TEST YOURSELF

1. What are the three main kingdoms of living things?
2. Why did biologists invent classification keys?

PLANTS

Another large group of living things is the plant kingdom. As with the animal kingdom, there is a huge variety, ranging from tiny, simple mosses to huge, complex plants, such as trees.

Plants use light, water, and carbon dioxide, a gas found in air, to make their own food. Plants that live on land usually get the water they need from the soil. Carbon dioxide and water are joined together to form food in a chemical process called photosynthesis. The food that a plant makes is a simple sugar called glucose.

For photosynthesis to occur, a plant must also have a source of energy. This energy is in the form of light from the sun. Some types of plant cells hold a chemical called chlorophyll which traps the sunlight. The energy is then used for photosynthesis.

Plants differ from animals in that all plants make their own food and all plant cells are inside a box-like cell wall made of a material called cellulose. Cell walls help to support the plant. Wood, for example, is basically made up of cell walls. Animals have soft, living cell walls.

The chart on the opposite page shows how biologists have classified the plant kingdom.

ACTIVITY

YOU NEED

- **3 small seedlings, each in a flower pot with a saucer**
- **a white plastic bag, pierced with small holes**

1 Place one of the seedlings on a well-lighted window sill. Water it.
2 Wrap another seedling in the white plastic bag. Make sure it has been watered.

3 Place the third seedling in a dark cupboard. Make sure that it has plenty of air, and water it.

4 Look at each seedling every day. Write down what happens to them. Make sure that their soil does not dry out.
5 When you begin to notice any changes in the two plants that do not have full light, put them out on the window sill with no covering. Continue observing them. What happens? Can you explain the results you observe?

TEST YOURSELF

1. What do plants need to make their own food?
2. For what do plants use chlorophyll?
3. What is the difference between plant and animal cells?

The Plant Kingdom

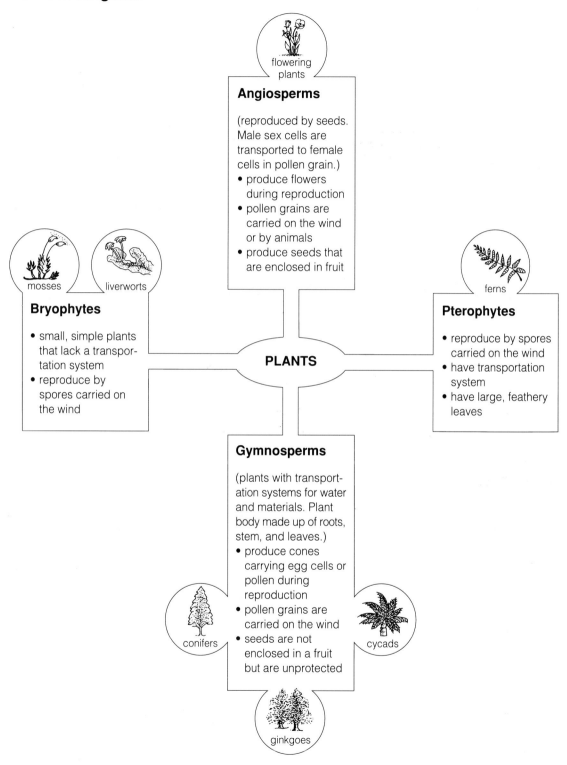

Angiosperms

(reproduced by seeds. Male sex cells are transported to female cells in pollen grain.)
- produce flowers during reproduction
- pollen grains are carried on the wind or by animals
- produce seeds that are enclosed in fruit

flowering plants

Bryophytes

- small, simple plants that lack a transportation system
- reproduce by spores carried on the wind

mosses   liverworts

PLANTS

Pterophytes

- reproduce by spores carried on the wind
- have transportation system
- have large, feathery leaves

ferns

Gymnosperms

(plants with transportation systems for water and materials. Plant body made up of roots, stem, and leaves.)
- produce cones carrying egg cells or pollen during reproduction
- pollen grains are carried on the wind
- seeds are not enclosed in a fruit but are unprotected

conifers   cycads   ginkgoes

DECOMPOSERS

What do you call a living thing that is rooted, has branches and cellulose cell walls, but is not green and cannot make its own food? In the past it was called a plant, but now biologists classify it in a kingdom of its own—the fungi. This group includes mushrooms, toadstools, and molds, such as the sort that you might find growing on a piece of old food.

Fungi are responsible for much of the waste disposal and recyling in nature, because they break down dead animal and plant remains. A fungus is made up of a network of fine threads, called the mycelium that spread over a large area of dead remains. The mycelium secretes chemicals that dissolve the dead material, turning it into a liquid. Then the mycelium absorbs the liquid as food. In this way, the piece of dead material gradually decomposes, or rots. Any part that is not used by the fungus goes back into the soil. Valuable nutrients, or food chemicals, are returned to the soil to be used by other living things that are present in nature.

When a fungus reaches a certain size, it produces special growths that release tiny, dustlike particles called spores. Each spore contains all the information that is needed to produce a new fungus of the same type. Large spore-producing growths are usually called mushrooms or toadstools. These large, fleshy growths are all we normally see of many types of fungus—the mycelium is usually under the surface of the food source.

This overripe fruit is gradually rotting as molds grow over the soft juicy flesh.

ACTIVITY

In this activity you are going to find out the best conditions for fungus growth. You are also going to find out whether fungus growth can be stopped or slowed down in any way.

WARNING: Never touch things that are rotting with your bare hands.

YOU NEED

- **toast**
- **dry bread**
- **damp bread**
- **a kitchen knife**
- **18 small self-sealing plastic bags**
- **labels**
- **vinegar**
- **sugar**
- **salt**
- **orange juice**
- **a hand lens**

1 Work in three groups.
2 Cut up 6 pieces of toast, 6 pieces of dry bread and 6 pieces of damp bread. Make sure they are all roughly the same size. Place each piece in a bag and seal. Label each dish: toast, dry bread, or damp bread.
3 Put a piece of toast in a dark cupboard. Put another piece of toast in a light place. Label your bags.

4 To each remaining piece of toast, add one of the following: vinegar, sugar, salt, and orange juice. Seal and label each bag. Set in the light.
5 Repeat steps 2 and 3 with the dry bread and the damp bread.
6 Leave the bags sealed for about a week. Use the hand lens to look through the bags and check for fungus.
7 Draw up a table for your results. In each space, write down a short description of each piece of toast, dry bread, or damp bread.

	dry bread	toast	damp bread
in dark			
in light			
+ vinegar			
+ sugar			
+ salt			
+ orange juice			

8 Which conditions were best for fungus growth? Which conditions helped to keep the food free of fungus?

TEST YOURSELF

1. How is a fungus different from a plant?
2. How do fungi get food?
3. What are mushrooms?

SIMPLE ANIMALS

There are several groups of animals that are very simple. Biologists use the word simple to mean living things whose bodies are collections of simple cells. These include jellyfish, sea anemones, corals, sponges, and some kinds of worms. If you look back at page 13, you will notice that all simple animals are invertebrates, or animals without backbones.

JELLYFISH, SEA ANEMONES, AND CORALS

This group of animals live in the ocean. Their bodies are very simple—two layers of cells surround a central tube, which is used for digesting food. The mouth is an opening at the top of the tube and is surrounded by tentacles which are used for feeding. Some animals have stinging cells in their tentacles that paralyze their prey.

Jellyfish swim after their food, while sea anemones and corals stay in one place and their food drifts past them. Corals live together in large groups called colonies. Each coral forms a hard substance around itself. After many years this substance builds up large underwater structures that are called coral reefs.

SPONGES

Sponges are similar to protists and jellyfish, but they live in colonies and build protective coverings much like those of coral. Sponges form three types of substances that they secrete. The lime sponges secrete limestone; Venus flower basket is built of silica; and the common bath sponge gets its protection from a horny material called spongin.

Coral in the Red Sea. Corals form hard outer skeletons in many different shapes and colors.

WORMS

There are several types of worms. Because they are made of three layers of cells, worms are slightly more advanced than jellyfish, sea anemones, corals, and sponges. Many worms have no gut or other internal organs—they take in food and oxygen and also get rid of wastes through their skin.

The simplest worms are the flatworms. Some are found in the ocean, in fresh water, and inside other animals. Many are parasites, such as the liver fluke and tapeworm, and cause serious diseases in humans and animals.

Most roundworms are also parasites. They include trichina worms and hookworm. Roundworms are more complex than flatworms, and have tough skins and long bodies with pointed ends.

The most complex worms are the annelids. They are also called segmented worms because their bodies are made up of many segments, or sections. These worms have a well-developed gut, a simple blood system, and a simple nervous system. The annelid with which you are probably most familiar is the earthworm, a very useful annelid that burrows in the soil and improves the soil's quality. Many annelids burrow on land. Some, such as the leech, live in fresh water. The leech feeds by sucking the blood of larger animals. Other annelids live in the ocean.

These diagrams show how an earthworm moves as it burrows in the soil.

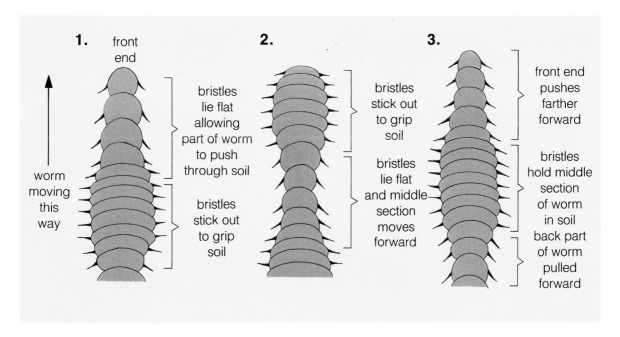

1. front end

bristles lie flat allowing part of worm to push through soil

bristles stick out to grip soil

worm moving this way

2. bristles stick out to grip soil

bristles lie flat and middle section moves forward

3. front end pushes farther forward

bristles hold middle section of worm in soil

back part of worm pulled forward

TEST YOURSELF

1. How do corals form reefs?
2. How does a sea anemone get its food?
3. What is an annelid?

MOLLUSKS

Mollusks make up a large and varied group with almost 80,000 different species. They can be found on land, in fresh water, and in the ocean—almost anywhere in the world. This is one reason why there are so many different kinds. All mollusks have soft bodies divided into two parts. There is a very soft part containing the mollusk's gut, lungs or gills, and brain. This part is usually protected by a shell, which is sometimes inside the body. The other part is the head-foot. This covers the very soft part and carries the eyes, mouth, and organs of movement.

There are three main groups of mollusks.

This giant clam is a bivalve. When it is open, water passes over the mollusk's food-filtering system which extracts tiny particles of food. If it senses danger, the clam slams its shells together.

GASTROPODS

Gastropods include snails, limpets, slugs, whelks, and sea slugs. They can be found on land, in the ocean and in fresh water. Most have coiled shells. The mouth has a tongue covered in teeth that are used for scraping food. All the land-living members of this group are herbivores—they eat plants. Some carnivorous gastropods live in the ocean.

BIVALVES

Bivalves are mollusks with two shells and no head. Most of them live in the ocean, although some live in fresh water. Some examples of bivalves are mussels, clams, oysters, and scallops. They are filter-feeders—they constantly take in water and filter out food particles.

CEPHALOPODS

The squid and octopus have a shell inside the body and belong to a group called cephalopods. This group lives in water and catches prey, such as crabs and lobsters. They are good swimmers, moving by a kind of jet propulsion. The head-foot has developed into a foot made up of eight or ten tentacles, or arms with rows of suckers that can hold prey. The head has a pair of powerful horny jaws, rather like a beak. They are used for tearing prey. Cephalopods have very good eyesight. Many can squirt out a jet of ink as a "smokescreen" when escaping from enemies. The cephalopods are the most intelligent of the invertebrate animals.

The common garden slug is a gastropod that lives on land and eats plants.

ACTIVITY

YOU NEED

- **a jar**
- **a garden snail or slug**
- **a flashlight**
- **different leaves**

1 Swirl a little water inside a jar to make it damp. Carefully place the snail or slug in the jar. Leave the jar alone until the snail or slug seems to have recovered from being moved.

2 Lift the jar gently and look at the underside of the animal. Look for the breathing holes. Can you see the mouth? Watch how it moves. Draw a picture to show what you see.

3 Shine the flashlight briefly on the snail or slug. What does it do?

4 Put some pieces of leaf in the jar with the snail or slug. What does it seem to like best?

5 When you have finished, return the garden snail or slug to the place where you found it.

TEST YOURSELF

1. Describe a snail's body.
2. How does a mussel get its food?
3. Why does an octopus sometimes squirt out ink?

ARTHROPODS

Arthropods make up the largest group of animals. So far scientists have classified one million different species of arthropods. And they estimate that there may be as many as 50 million species altogether. The variety in the group is astonishing—ranging from ants, bees, and butterflies to crabs and shrimp. They have jointed limbs arranged in pairs. (The word arthropod means jointed foot). Some of these limbs are adapted for getting food. Their bodies are divided into segments and are covered by the cuticle, a hard outer layer. The cuticle forms an outer skeleton and protects the animal's body.

INSECTS

Insects are the largest, and most successful, group of arthropods. Not only can insects eat almost anything and live almost anywhere except the ocean, they are the only invertebrates that can fly. Because they are able to fly, they are able to escape from other animals and can find new habitats and new sources of food. And because

their cuticle is waterproof, the body of an insect does not dry out. This enables insects to live in very hot, dry places.

The body of an adult insect is divided into three main segments—the head, thorax, and abdomen. The head has eyes, antennae, and a mouth. In those insects that fly, one or two pairs of wings are attached to the thorax. All insects have three pairs of legs attached to the thorax. The abdomen contains all the other main body organs.

One problem for insects is the cuticle—an insect cannot grow larger than its hard outer skeleton. Some insects overcome this problem by molting. They hatch from their eggs as tiny, wingless adults. As they grow larger, they split and shed their cuticles. This uncovers their soft bodies, and they often hide until the new, larger cuticle has hardened. These insects go through

Treehoppers are insects that undergo metamorphosis. The small white ones are larvae, the yellow ones are adults that have just emerged from the chrysalis and the black ones are older adults.

24

several molts before they reach the full-grown adult size.

The other way of solving the growth problem is by metamorphosis. This word means changing shape, and that is exactly what the insect does. The young insect hatches out as a larva with a soft, wormlike body. It eats vast amounts of food. When it reaches a certain size, it goes into a resting stage; for instance, a butterfly larva becomes a chrysalis. This is covered with a hard, protective layer. The insect's body rearranges itself inside the chrysalis. When it is ready, the insect breaks out as a fully grown adult. All moths and butterflies have a life cycle like this. Some insects, such as mosquitoes, depend on water for the larval stage. However, they all breathe in the same way—oxygen is taken in through holes, called spiracles, in the sides of the body.

Some insects such as ants, bees, and termites, live in large groups called colonies, building large, specialized nests. Each member of the colony has its own job, such as collecting food, making tunnels, or tending the young.

SPIDERS

Many people think that spiders are insects, but they are not. Unlike insects, spiders have four pairs of legs, and they never have wings. Spiders produce silk from several pairs of structures on the abdomen called spinnerets.

A spider's body is divided into two main parts: the head-thorax and the abdomen. The mouth and eyes are at the front of the head-thorax, while the legs and stomach are at the back. The abdomen contains all the other major body organs, such as the heart, lung, and ovary.

Most spiders use poison to stun or kill their prey, and they use their silk in different ways. They may use their silk to build webs, to wrap their prey, or as a drop line for diving.

Spiders use their silk in many different ways to trap prey and to protect their young. The net-casting spider spins a web that it throws at its prey. The prey becomes entangled in the sticky silk net and the spider moves in for the kill.

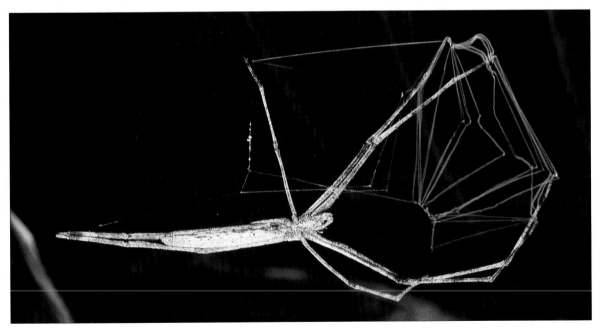

Soldier crabs feeding on the sand of an Australian shore. Crabs are crustaceans. They are found on shores all around the world, and in the depths of the sea.

CRUSTACEANS

Most crustaceans live in water and include lobsters, crabs, and shrimp. Their cuticle forms a very hard shell from which they molt as they grow. The body is divided into two main parts—the head-thorax and the abdomen. Unlike spiders or insects, crustaceans have five pairs of legs attached to the thorax. The first pair serves as large claws. Smaller legs, called swimmerets are attached to the abdomen.

CENTIPEDES AND MILLIPEDES

These animals get their names from their large numbers of legs ("centi" means hundred and "milli" means thousand). A centipede may have from fifteen to 100 segments to its body, with one pair of legs on each segment. Centipedes move very quickly and many have a poisonous bite used for killing small insects. There are thousands of species of centipedes.

Millipedes have wormlike bodies. They have two pairs of legs on each segment, but move very slowly compared with centipedes. When a millipede is in danger, it does not run away, but rolls itself up into a ball. Millipedes eat plants, and they do not have poison.

ACTIVITY

1 Get permission to go to a garden, park, or woods. Look under stones and pieces of wood or bark and collect anything that you think is an arthropod. Watch out for poisonous plants and stinging insects.

2 Pick up the animals very gently with tweezers and place them in the jars. Look at them with the hand lens.

3 Use the classification key to help you to name your arthropod.

4 Draw up a chart to show how many of each arthropod you found, and where you found them.

5 Replace all your arthropods where you found them when you have finished your study.

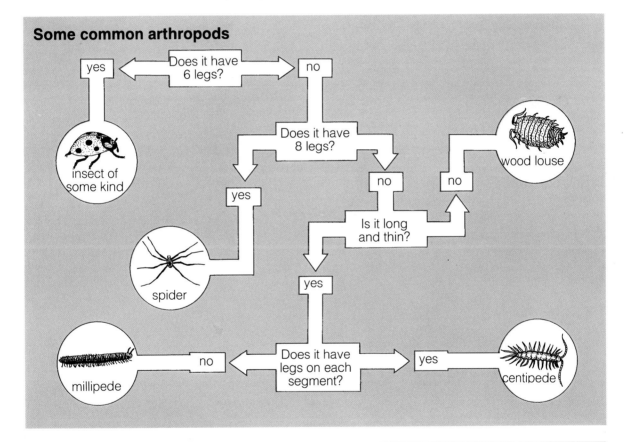

Some common arthropods

Does it have 6 legs? — yes → insect of some kind

Does it have 6 legs? — no → Does it have 8 legs?

Does it have 8 legs? — yes → spider

Does it have 8 legs? — no → Is it long and thin?

Is it long and thin? — no → wood louse

Is it long and thin? — yes → Does it have legs on each segment?

Does it have legs on each segment? — no → millipede

Does it have legs on each segment? — yes → centipede

TEST YOURSELF

1. What does the word arthropod means?

2. How is a spider different from an insect?

3. What is metamorphosis?

WARNING: Never go to parks or woods alone. Always tell an adult where you are going.

FISH

Fish were the first vertebrates, or animals with backbones to appear on Earth. With almost 23,000 species, they are the largest group of vertebrates. Fish can be found in the ocean and in fresh water and at a large range of depths and temperatures.

Most fish are streamlined, or shaped to easily glide through the water. Scales covering the body help to streamline and protect the fish. As the fish swims, water flows over its gills. Blood passing through the gills picks up oxygen from the water and carries the oxygen to all parts of the body. Fish do not control their body temperature—it goes up and down with the water temperature. Most fish lay eggs from which tiny fish hatch and swim away. A few species, such as the sea horse, look after their young.

There is an enormous variety of fish, ranging from the tiny neon-tetra to huge sharks. And there is a wide range of shapes from the sea horse to the snake-like eel. However, all fish have the same general body plan, as shown below.

There are three main groups of fish. The most primitive are the jawless fish such as the lamprey and hagfish. The cartilaginous fish, such as sharks and rays, have skeletons made of cartilage. Touch your nose to find out what cartilage feels like. It is not easy for these fish to make sudden stops and turns.

Bony fish make up the largest and most complex group of fish. As their name suggests, this type of fish has a bony skeleton. Some examples of bony fish are cod, carp, sea horse, bass, trout, and salmon. Most of the fish that we eat belong to this group, including cod, flounder, perch, bass, catfish, tuna, herring, and bluefish. Bony fish swim well and can turn and stop easily.

Scientists are especially interested in one group of bony fish, called the lobe-finned fish. In addition to gills, these fish have a simple type of lung. They can breathe air and can briefly leave the water and go on land. Scientists believe that the ancestors of lobe-finned fish are also the ancestors of amphibians.

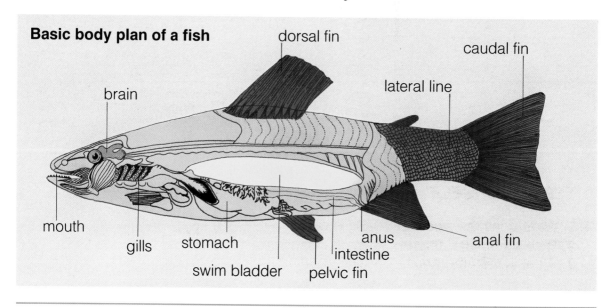

Basic body plan of a fish — dorsal fin, caudal fin, brain, lateral line, mouth, gills, stomach, swim bladder, intestine, pelvic fin, anus, anal fin

This sea horse is an unusual kind of bony fish. Bony fish are the most advanced fish.

ACTIVITY

YOU NEED

- **a whole, fresh trout or other fish from a market**
- **a cutting board**
- **sharp scissors**
- **a scalpel**
- **tweezers**

1 Ask an adult to cut up the fish carefully as shown in the diagram.
2 Use the diagram on page 28 to help you find the gills, brain, intestines, fins, and skeleton. You may also find some eggs in the female fish.

TEST YOURSELF

1. What are the three main groups of fish?
2. How do fish get oxygen from water?
3. How do lobe-finned fish differ from other fish?

AMPHIBIANS AND REPTILES

AMPHIBIANS

Amphibians make up a small group of vertebrates with just over 4,000 different species. This group includes frogs and toads (the largest group of amphibians), salamanders, and newts. Even though amphibians are more advanced than fish, both groups are cold-blooded—they do not control their body temperature.

Although the adults live on land, amphibians are dependent on water. They breed in water, laying jelly-like eggs. These hatch out into tadpoles, which breathe through gills. Tadpoles change shape gradually, growing legs and developing lungs to replace the gills. This process is called metamorphosis or a series of changes in form that the organism undergoes. Eventually, they move onto land, where they breathe using their lungs. Most amphibians also breathe through their skin, which is smooth and moist. If its skin dries out, this type of amphibian will die.

This female arrow poison frog is carrying a tadpole on her back. The moist air of the rain forest where she lives will keep the tadpole from drying out.

REPTILES

There are about 5,200 species of reptiles alive today. There are four main groups—snakes, lizards, turtles and tortoises, and crocodiles and alligators. Snakes and lizards make up the largest groups. Reptiles are related to amphibians, but are more advanced. Reptiles were the first true land vertebrates. They have well-developed lungs, which they use all the time. Even those that spend much of their lives in water, such as crocodiles, water snakes, and turtles, must return to the surface to breathe.

Reptiles are cold-blooded. Most of them live in warm countries—the heat allows them to stay active for much of the day.

A young Brazilian alligator basking in the sun. Reptiles do this to raise their body temperature.

Their dry, scaly skin prevents water loss, allowing reptiles to live and thrive in very dry areas.

Reptiles lay their eggs on land. The eggs have hard or leathery waterproof shells. They look like tiny adults when they hatch. Only a few species look after their young.

Snakes do not have legs and most move by curving back and forth and pushing themselves forward. Most snakes lay their eggs, but some give birth to live young that hatch out of eggs inside the mother. As snakes grow, they molt their skins.

Many snakes, such as vipers, have poison fangs with which they kill their prey. Others such as the boa constrictor, can crush their prey to death. Snakes swallow their prey whole after they have killed it. Many snakes, such as garter snakes, are not poisonous and do not harm humans.

Lizards live in many different places and are usually quite small. They do not have poison. They eat insects, which they catch using long, sticky tongues.

Turtles and tortoises are a very unusual and ancient group. They have a hard shell, which is the backbone and the ribs joined together in a special hard growth. A tortoise or turtle can withdraw its head, two pairs of legs, and tail into its shell for protection. Tortoises are land animals. They move very slowly and are herbivores. Many turtles swim well and fast. They are mostly carnivorous.

Crocodiles and alligators are the largest reptiles. They are very good swimmers and spend most of their lives in water. They are all fierce hunters and are completely carnivorous.

TEST YOURSELF

1. How do tadpoles breathe?
2. Describe how a baby amphibian turns into an adult.
3. How do reptiles that spend most of their time in water breathe?
4. Snakes have no legs. How do they move?

BIRDS

There are about 8600 species of birds living today, divided into twenty-seven different orders. Birds descended from reptiles and are among the most highly developed animals. Birds have one great advantage over reptiles and most other vertebrates—they are warm-blooded. This means that they have a constant body temperature. They use some of the energy from their food to keep this temperature the same all the time. An animal that is warm-blooded can be active when the weather is cold and, therefore, can live in very cold places. Birds are covered with feathers, which also help reduce heat loss, especially during flight.

The ability to fly is another reason for the success of birds. Flight is useful because the animal can move over great distances to find food. It can also escape enemies. Many birds migrate—avoiding the cold weather and food shortages. The front limbs of a bird are adapted to form wings with very strong muscles at the shoulder. Its bones are hollow, making it light. Some birds, such as the penguin, ostrich, emu, and rhea, are the exception to the rule and cannot fly.

Birds eat a wide range of foods. For example, hummingbirds sip nectar; parrots, finches and canaries eat seeds; and swallows eat insects. Eagles and hawks eat rodents and rabbits, while pelicans eat fish. Beaks are adapted to the bird's food—some can break seeds while others scoop up fish. A bird has no teeth. It swallows gravel, which it stores in its gizzard. This grinds up the food. It also has a food storage organ called the crop.

Birds lay eggs covered by hard shells. Almost all birds look after their young in nests of various types. They use their body heat to keep the eggs warm. After the young have hatched, the parents look after them until they can fly and find food for themselves.

Some baby birds need more care than others. For example, chickens are born with feathers and are able to run around right away. Others, such as the baby robin, are featherless and helpless right after their birth.

When the chicks of domestic chickens hatch, they are already covered with feathers and are able to run around. Chicks from many other species are born without feathers and helpless.

Emperor penguins in Antarctica. Penguins cannot fly, they use their wings as paddles for swimming.

ACTIVITY

INVESTIGATING FEATHERS

YOU NEED

- **several feathers**
- **a hand lens**
- **a plastic bowl filled with water**
- **some oil (vegetable oil is safest)**
- **rubber gloves**
- **some dish-washing liquid**

1 Look carefully at a feather under the hand lens. Draw what you see.

2 Drop the feather into the bowl of water. Does it float? Pick it up. What happens to the water on the feather?

3 Dip the feather into the vegetable oil. Now repeat step 2. What happens? What does it look like?

4 Pour some dish-washing liquid into the bowl of water and mix. Remember to wear rubber gloves. Wash the oily feather thoroughly and let it dry. Then repeat step 2. What happens?

5 Find out what happens to birds that get caught in oil spills at sea and how they can be rescued. Do your results agree with what you have found out?

TEST YOURSELF

1. What are the advantages of being able to fly?
2. Birds have no teeth. How do they grind up their food?
3. How is a bird's body adapted for flight?

MAMMALS

Mammals are a very highly developed group of animals. There are about 4,000 different species, living almost everywhere on Earth. They all breathe using lungs—even those that live in the ocean, such as whales, must return to the surface to breathe.

Mammals are the only animals that have hair or fur and that feed their young with milk produced in special glands in the mother's body. Mammals tend to have very few babies at one time. The babies usually develop inside the mother and are not hatched from eggs. Like birds, all mammals are warm-blooded. Hair and fur hold in body heat. Some mammals lower their body temperature by sweating, while others pant to get rid of excess body heat.

EGG-LAYING MAMMALS

There are only two species of this type of mammal—the duck-billed platypus and the spiny anteater. They are the most primitive mammals. Although they lay eggs, they feed their young on milk.

MARSUPIALS

These mammals live mainly in Australia, although some can be found in the Americas. They give birth to tiny, hairless, blind babies. The baby crawls into its mother's pouch and attaches itself to a nipple where it takes in milk until it is fully developed. Some examples of marsupials are the kangaroo, koala, and opossum.

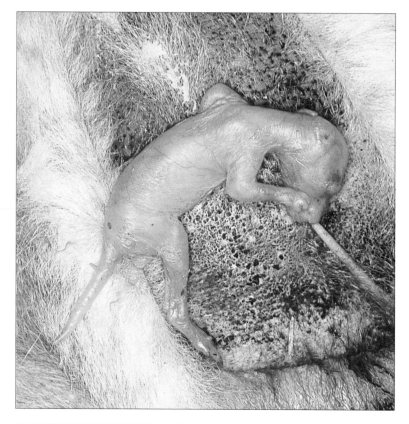

A baby kangaroo leaves its mother's womb while it is still very undeveloped. It crawls into the mother's pouch and attaches itself to a special tube, through which it sucks milk.

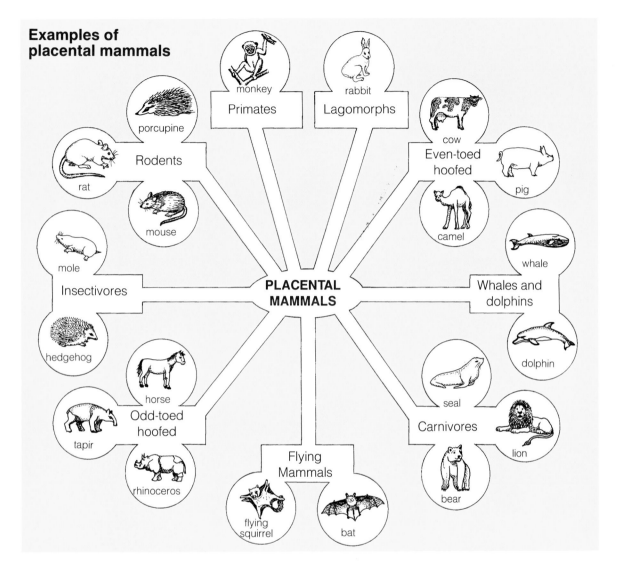

Examples of placental mammals

porcupine
Rodents
rat
mouse
monkey
Primates
rabbit
Lagomorphs
cow
Even-toed hoofed
pig
camel
whale
Whales and dolphins
dolphin
mole
Insectivores
hedgehog
PLACENTAL MAMMALS
seal
Carnivores
lion
horse
Odd-toed hoofed
tapir
rhinoceros
Flying Mammals
flying squirrel
bat
bear

PLACENTAL MAMMALS

Placental mammals are highly developed and include more species than the other two groups. Many intelligent animals, including humans, belong to this group. Placental mammals develop in a special organ inside the mother's body. This organ is called the uterus. The developing young get food and oxygen from the mother through another special organ called the placenta, which develops inside the mother's uterus. The placenta also takes waste away from the baby. The baby stays inside its mother for a long developing time called the gestation period.

At birth, some placental mammals, such as mice and humans, are helpless. Others, such as cattle and sheep, can walk shortly after birth. However, all these mammals stay with their mothers until they are old enough to care for themselves. The amount of protection that is given to the young before and after birth is one of the reasons for the success of placental mammals. The chart shows nine different groups of placental mammals, as diverse as the porcupine and the camel.

THE HUMAN ANIMAL

Humans belong to the group of placental mammals called primates. This advanced and intelligent group of animals all have large brains. The group includes lemurs, marmosets, monkeys, apes, gorillas, chimpanzees, and many others. Although humans are not descended from the same kinds of apes that you find in the zoo, humans and apes share a common ancestor. Apes, monkeys, and humans all evolved, or changed, differently over time.

Most primates have thumbs that work in the opposite direction to the fingers. This is very useful, because it forms a hand that can grip firmly and make complicated movements, such as using a tool. All primates have both eyes on the front of the head and similar teeth. Most primates are omnivorous, which means they eat meat and plants. Some, like the gorilla, are mainly vegetarian.

One difference between humans and other primates is that humans walk upright, leaving the front limbs free for other tasks. But the main difference between humans and other primates is the ability to use complex thought, such as language. When humans first appeared on Earth, they were not very different from other mammals in the way they lived. They were not as strong, nor did they move as quickly as many others, but they used their intelligence to develop weapons and to hunt in groups. This meant that they could hunt and kill animals that were much larger and stronger than themselves. Humans have continued to use their intelligence and have become the dominant species on Earth.

Humans and hamsters are both placental mammals. Humans are primates, the most advanced and intelligent group of placental mammals.

Different animals tending their young

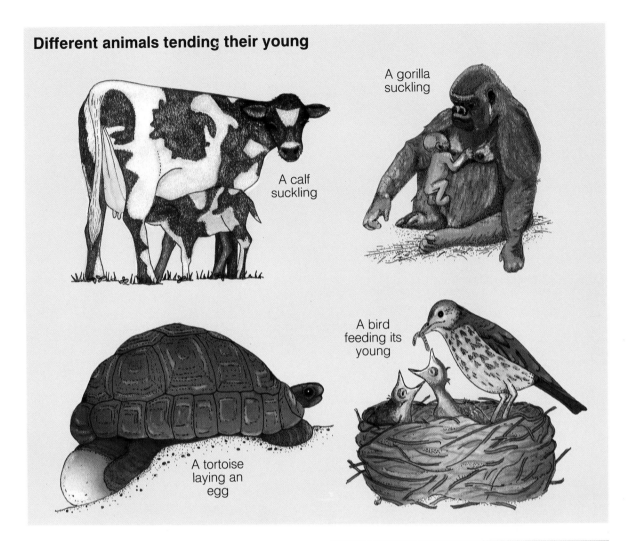

A gorilla suckling

A calf suckling

A bird feeding its young

A tortoise laying an egg

ACTIVITY

Look carefully at the pictures of different animals tending their young. Make a chart with 4 columns, as shown. Put a check in the right column for each animal. The animals with checks in the last two columns are all mammals.

	lays eggs	has hair	feeds young on milk
name of animal			

TEST YOURSELF

1. List three things that all mammals have in common.
2. What are marsupials?
3. To which order of mammals do humans belong?

EVOLUTION AND EXTINCTION

You have looked at some examples of the variety of life on our planet. Scientists have discovered that this variety has changed dramatically over millions of years. Once-successful animals, such as dinosaurs, are extinct (have completely died out), while others have close relatives living today.

You may wonder how we know about living things that are no longer found on the Earth. It is because they have left traces of themselves in the rocks. These remains are called fossils.

A fossil is the remains of a living thing from the distant past. Most fossils consist of bones and shells that have been changed into rocklike substances over

millions of years. Others are little more than impressions, or casts, in fine-grained rocks. Even the footprints of extinct animals are fossils.

The fossil record has may gaps—partly because so few animals and plants became fossilized and partly because it is impossible to find all the fossils buried in the rocks. However, enough remains have been found for scientists to find out when, how, and why many different life-forms changed and developed. This process of change is called evolution. The chart shows the most important events in the history of evolution.

How does evolution happen? We can never be sure exactly how a particular

The record in the rocks

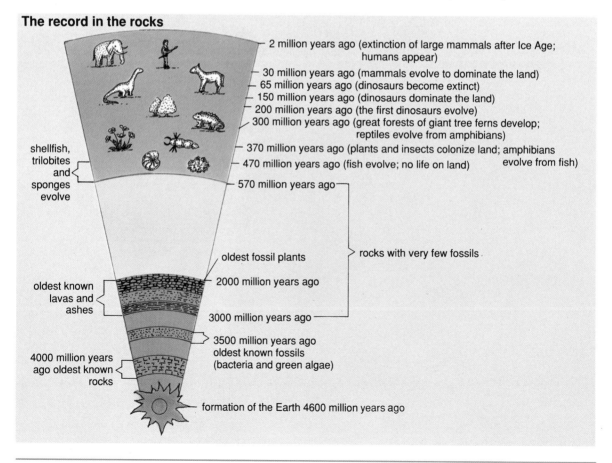

- 2 million years ago (extinction of large mammals after Ice Age; humans appear)
- 30 million years ago (mammals evolve to dominate the land)
- 65 million years ago (dinosaurs become extinct)
- 150 million years ago (dinosaurs dominate the land)
- 200 million years ago (the first dinosaurs evolve)
- 300 million years ago (great forests of giant tree ferns develop; reptiles evolve from amphibians)
- 370 million years ago (plants and insects colonize land; amphibians evolve from fish)
- 470 million years ago (fish evolve; no life on land)
- 570 million years ago

shellfish, trilobites and sponges evolve

rocks with very few fossils

oldest fossil plants

oldest known lavas and ashes

2000 million years ago

3000 million years ago

4000 million years ago oldest known rocks

3500 million years ago oldest known fossils (bacteria and green algae)

formation of the Earth 4600 million years ago

Giraffes probably evolved their long necks at a time when competition for food by plant-eaters was fierce. Any animal with a slightly longer neck could get food that other herbivores could not reach.

species of plant or animal has evolved but there are a few general rules we can follow.

At some time in the distant past, a population of animals or plants becomes divided by a barrier—perhaps by a sea or a range of mountains. This stops the two groups from breeding together. Each group now has its own environment—perhaps with a different climate. Each group must try to adapt. This means they must change to cope with new conditions.

If the two groups manage to survive, they may develop quite differently. This process may take millions of years. Eventually, the two groups may become so different that they would not be able to breed, even if they could meet. This means that there are now two species instead of one— and more variety has been introduced.

A process called natural selection works here. Natural selection is the constant struggle to survive that goes on among living things. If some members of a species vary from the others in a useful way, they will tend to survive. They will produce young that also have these useful variations. Those that cannot adapt will die. Sometimes, a whole species cannot adapt to its new environment. When a whole species dies out, it is called extinction.

Sometimes, whole groups of living things become extinct. This is what happened to the dinosaurs. No one knows exactly why this sort of large scale extinction happened. It is most likely to have been caused by a sudden change in the climate.

Extinction is not just something that happened millions of years ago. You may have heard of a bird called the dodo. This bird lived on the island of Mauritius in the Indian Ocean. When Dutch sailors arrived there in the early 1600s, they quickly

discovered that the dodo was a good source of food. The bird was clumsy and could not fly, so it was easy to catch. It was hunted to extinction by the end of the seventeenth century.

Species are becoming extinct even today. This is mostly because of humans. Some species have been hunted to extinction or near-extinction for the sport of it or for food. This has happened to many whales, and there is now an international ban on whaling to protect the species that are left.

Many habitats have been polluted or destroyed by building, farming, mining, or by other industries. For example, ancient forests in Oregon and Washington, in the

Above *An artist's impression of a dodo, a bird that has been extinct for nearly 300 years.*

Right *This jaguar lives in the wilds of the Amazon rain forest. It is a threatened species as its habitat is gradually being destroyed by human activity.*

Pacific Northwest, are being cut down to make paper. Forest destruction has led to the spotted owl being listed by the government as an endangered species. The only way in which the spotted owl and many other species will survive is if large areas of forest are left untouched. Human activity often changes a habitat much too fast for any species to be able to adapt and survive in that habitat.

Like the spotted owl, the woolly spider monkey from southeast Brazil has joined the list of endangered species. Its home in the rain forest is being destroyed by humans. The orangutan of Sumatra is yet another endangered species.

ACTIVITY

INVESTIGATING ENDANGERED ANIMALS

You are going to make a card index of animals that are in danger of extinction. A card index is a set of cards with information, arranged in alphabetical, or other, order.

1 Choose some animals from the list below. These are all endangered species.

blue whale	spotted owl
Beluga whale	osprey
pilot whale	California condor
white rhinoceros	

2 Write the name of each animal on a separate card. Then put the headings as shown in the example.

YOU NEED

- **index cards or blank cards that will fit into the box (can be cut from thin cardboard)**
- **a box (a small child's shoe box is ideal)**
- **access to a library**

Blue whale

numbers before whaling
numbers today
what is being done to stop extinction

3 Arrange the cards in alphabetical order in your box.
4 Find out the information about each endangered animal in your card index. A good library will be helpful.
5 Find out about some more endangered species and add them to your card index. You may find out even more about them on television or in newspapers and magazines.

TEST YOURSELF

1. Why does the fossil record have so many gaps?
2. What is natural selection?
3. List three ways in which humans can cause species to become endangered or extinct.

41

GENETICS

You have seen how the environment can affect evolution and can increase the variety of life. But why does evolution happen? What causes changes in living things to take place? The answer lies within the cells of living things.

Look at your family. You can probably see some similarities between different members of your family—perhaps you have the same eye color as your mother, or the same type of nose as your father. If you look at your grandparents, you will see similar characteristics in them. We say that you have inherited these particular characteristics.

When living things breed, they pass on a set of chemical instructions. These instructions direct the growth of the new individual, or the offspring. Consider yourself as an example. Your body is made up of billions of tiny cells. Each one contains the chemical instructions that have passed from your parents to you. One cell from your father, called the sperm, contained half the instructions. The other half came from your mother's cell—the egg. All the chemical instructions you needed were laid down when the egg, or female sex cell, and the sperm, or male sex cell, joined together.

Human offspring inherit characteristics from both parents.

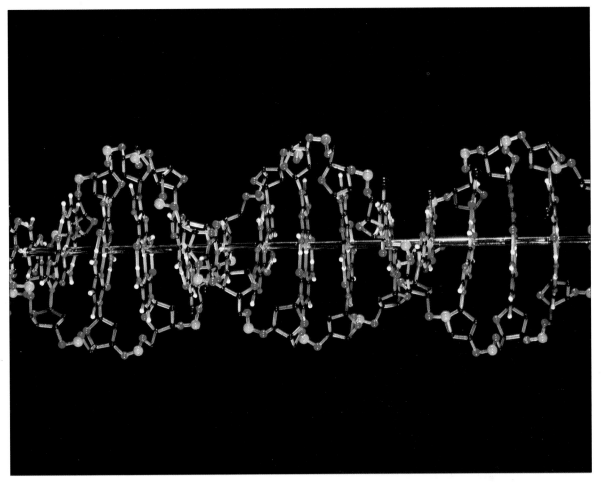

This is a model of the chemical that passes on instructions in living things. The chemical is called DNA, and it makes up genetic material.

These instructions are given by chemical codes called genes. There are millions of genes in each of your cells. Since these genes come from your parents, it is not surprising that you inherit a mixture of their characteristics.

If you have brothers or sisters, you may wonder why they do not look exactly like you. It is because your parents' genes can be put together in different ways when eggs and sperm are formed. A simple example may help to explain how this happens. Take two sentences:

- **The dog eats a bone**
- **The cat sits on a chair**

These are the "parent" sentences. Now jumble them up to make new sentences— the "offspring" sentences. For example:

- **The cat eats a bone**
- **The dog sits on a chair**
- **The cat eats a chair**
- **The cat sits on a bone**

You can see that all the "offspring" sentences have characteristics from both "parent" sentences. However, none of the "offspring" sentences is exactly alike—they all have different meanings.

So, with each new generation, there is a slight change—more variety is introduced into the species.

This is not the only way in which variety and change is caused in a species. Sometimes, a mistake occurs in one or more of the genes, and this may alter the way in which the gene behaves. A genetic mistake is called a mutation. Many mutations are harmless; some are harmful and may cause death, while others can be useful, perhaps even good for the species.

When a mutation is useful, it improves the life of the offspring in some way. When it breeds, it produces more offspring—some with the mutation. These may eventually take over as the new form of the species. Scientists believe that this is the main cause of evolution.

Not all mutations are good for a living thing. In humans, for example, there are some very serious diseases that are caused by genetic mutations and are inherited. One is hemophilia, a disease in which a person cannot stop bleeding when cut or bruised. Another inherited disease is cystic fibrosis. This disease affects babies or young children, causing serious difficulties in digesting food and breathing. Severe cases of cystic fibrosis can cause death after a few years. Scientists are now developing special genetic tests. These tests can tell people whether or not they are likely to have children with these and other serious inherited diseases.

Two different forms of the same species of moth—the peppered moth. The black form (above) is a mutation and was once rare. However, the Industrial Revolution arrived and tree trunks blackened because of pollution. The normal pale moths (below) became easy prey for birds. The black moths were well camouflaged against the dirty tree trunks, so they were not so easily picked off by birds. The black moths were better able to survive and pass on their mutated gene, so they became much more common. This is a good example of a useful genetic mutation.

ACTIVITY

MAKING AN INHERITANCE CHART

YOU NEED

- **a stiff piece of cardboard**
- **some colored pens**

- **information about members of your family**

---

1 Make a family tree. Use the example shown to help you.

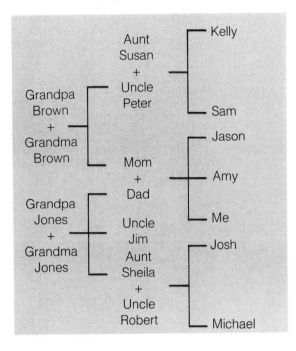

Key: eye color — fair skin, burns easily in sun **F**; hair color — skin does not burn easily in sun **B**

2 Choose different characteristics: for example, hair color (you will have to ask much older family members what color hair they had when they were young), eye color, and height. Make a list of them for each member of the family that you have included.

3 Make a key for each characteristic. Some examples are shown to help you. Mark each family member's characteristics on the family tree.

4 Can you see how different characteristics have been passed on?

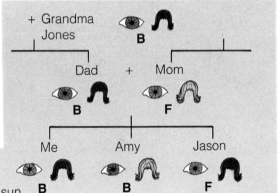

TEST YOURSELF

1. What is mutation?
2. How do you inherit characteristics from your parents?
3. Can you think of any diseases that are not inherited?
Try to explain your answer.

Glossary

Abdomen   The part of the body below the chest; the last part of the body of an arthropod.

Carnivore   An animal that eats only meat.

Cast   A molded shape; a fossil having the same outer shape as the plant or animal that formed it.

Cell   A small unit of living material.

Chrysalis   The silky case or cocoon that an insect larva makes around itself before it turns into an adult.

Colonies   Large groups of living things that live together in one place.

Dominant   The most influential living thing in a particular group. Humans are said to be the dominant animal species in the world.

Environment   The surroundings of a living thing.

Gestation   The period of time when the offspring of a mammal is developing inside its mother.

Habitat   The natural home of a living thing.

Herbivore   An animal that eats only plants.

Host   (in biology) An animal or plant that provides food and protection for a parasite.

Metamorphosis   The change of an animal larva into the adult form, such as a tadpole into a frog.

Migrate   To travel to different habitats at certain times of the year. Birds and fish are examples of animals that migrate.

Molting   Shedding skin, feathers, fur, or cuticle.

Nipple   A small projection on a mammal's body from which a baby mammal can suck milk.

Organs   Parts of a living thing that carry out vital tasks. An example is the heart.

Parasite   A living thing that lives in or on another living thing (the host). The parasite benefits, while the host is harmed.

Placenta   An organ through which a placental mammal receives food and gets rid of wastes before birth.

Prey   An animal hunted or caught by another animal for food.

Raw materials   Natural substances from the Earth (from the land, sea, or air) which are used to make other products. For example, wood is a raw material used to make paper; food is a raw material used by living things for growth, energy, and health.

Recycling   Breaking down a substance to make a new one. Reusing waste material.

Secrete   To give out. For example, humans secrete sweat.

Segments   Sections.

Silica   A hard material that does not dissolve in water. It is made from silicon and oxygen.

Species   A group of living things that can breed together to produce offspring.

Termite   A white, ant-like insect.

Thorax   The chest region.

Uterus   An organ in which the baby of a placental mammal develops before birth.

Books to Read

Bender, Lionel. *Simple Creatures.* Franklin Watts, 1988

Benton, Michael. *The Story of Life on Earth,* Watts, 1986.

Berman, William. *How to Dissect.* 4th ed. Prentice Hall, 1984

Biology Encyclopedia, Checkerboard, 1989

Book of Mammals, 2 vols. National Geographic, 1981

Claridge, Marit and Shackell, John. *Living Things: A Simple Introduction.* Educational Development Corporation, 1986

Corrick, James A. *Recent Revolutions in Biology,* Watts, 1987

Edelson, Edward. *Genetics and Heredity.* Chelsea, 1986

Oda, Hidetomo. *Snails.* Raintree Steck-Vaughn, 1986

O'Neill, Mary. *Life After the Dinosaurs,* Troll, 1989

Picture Acknowledgments

The authors would like to thank the following for allowing illustrations to be reproduced in this book: Bruce Coleman *cover* (top/Kjell B. Sanved/Photo Researcher), 25 (M.P.L. Fogden), 29 (Jane Burton); Oxford Scientific Films *cover* (below right/Larry Crowhurst), *frontispiece* (Michael Fogden), 7 (bottom right/Sean Morris), 8 (Martin Colbeck), 12 (G.I. Bernard), 22 (Fredrick Ehrenstrom), 24 (Michael Fogden), 25 (M.P.L. Fogden), 26, 30 (Michael Fogden), 33 (Kjell Sandved), 34 (Root), 44 (Peter Parks/both); Wayland Picture Library 6 (Trevor Hill), 7 (left), 9, 10 (Colin S. Milkins), 15 (Sarah McKenzie), 18 (Zul Mukhida), 20, 23 (Sarah McKenzie), 31 (Julia Waterlow), 32, 36 (Zul Mukhida), 39, 40 (Julia Waterlow), 42 (Zul Mukhida); Zefa 43. All artwork is by Marilyn Clay.

Index

Adaptation 39
Algae 10, 11
Amphibians 30, 31
Animals 6, 7, 10, 12, 16, 20, 21, 24, 26, 30, 32, 34, 36, 37, 39
Arthropods 12, 24-27
Australia 26, 34

Backbone 12, 20
Bacteria 6, 10, 12
Birds 15, 32–33
Birth 34, 35
Blood 21, 30
Bony fish 28
Brain 22, 36

Carbon dioxide 16
Carnivores 12, 22
Cartilaginous fish 28
Cells 10, 16, 20, 21, 42, 43
Cellulose 16, 18
Centipedes 26
Climate 39, 40
Cold-blooded 30
Corals 20, 21
Crustaceans 26

Decomposers 18-19
Dinosaurs 38, 39
Diseases 10, 44

Egg 8, 24, 30, 32, 34, 42, 43
Egg-laying mammals 34
Energy 6, 7, 9, 16, 32
Environment 39, 42
Evolution 38-41, 42, 44
Extinction 38-41
Eyes 22, 24, 25, 36

Filter-feeders 22
Fish 28-29
Flight 24, 32

Food 6, 7, 10, 16, 18, 20, 21, 22, 24, 25, 26, 32, 35
Fossils 38
Fresh water 21, 22, 28
Fungi 12, 18-19

Genes 43, 44
Gestation 35
Gills 22, 26, 28
Growth 6, 7, 24, 25

Habitats 40
Head 22, 23, 36
Herbivores 22
Humans 35, 36

Insects 24-25, 26, 32
Intelligence 23, 35, 36
Invertebrates 12, 13, 23

Jawless fish 28
Jellyfish 20

Land 22, 28
Larva 25
Legs 12, 24, 25, 26
Limbs 24, 26, 32
Lobe-fins 28
Lungs 22, 34

Mammals 12, 34-37
Marsupials 34
Metamorphosis 25
Millipedes 12, 26
Mollusks 22-23
Mouth 20, 22, 24, 25
Mutation 44

Natural selection 39

Ocean 20, 21, 22, 24, 28, 34
Offspring 42, 43, 44
Omnivorous 36

Oxygen 6, 10, 21, 25, 35

Parasite 10, 21
Photosynthesis 16
Placenta 35
Placental mammals 35, 36
Plants 6, 7, 10, 12, 16-17, 18, 22, 26, 36, 39
Prey 23, 25

Reproduction 8
Reptiles 30-31
Respiration 6, 7, 9

Sea anemones 20, 21
Shell 22, 23, 26, 32, 38
Skeleton 24
Skin 12, 21, 34
Soil 10, 16, 18
Species 8, 24, 30, 35, 39, 40, 43, 44
Sperm 8, 42, 43
Spiders 12, 25
Sponges 20, 21
Spores 18
Streamlining 28
Sweating 34

Tadpoles 30
Teeth 22, 32, 36
Thorax 24

Uterus 35

Vertebrates 12, 14, 28, 32

Warm-blooded 12, 32, 34
Waste 7, 10, 21, 35
Water 10, 16, 21, 22, 23, 24, 26, 28
Wings 24, 32
Worms 20, 21

Young 8

First published in 1992 by Wayland (Publishers) Ltd.
© Copyright 1992 Wayland (Publishers) Ltd.